LUNAR

LUNAR

CHRIS BRADFORD

Illustrated by
Charlotte Grange

Barrington Stoke

Published by Barrington Stoke
An imprint of HarperCollins*Publishers*
Westerhill Road, Bishopbriggs, Glasgow, G64 2QT

www.barringtonstoke.co.uk

HarperCollins*Publishers*
Macken House, 39/40 Mayor Street Upper,
Dublin 1, DO1 C9W8, Ireland

First published in 2023

ISBN 978-1-80090-229-9

10 9 8 7 6 5 4 3 2

Printed and bound in India by Replika Press Pvt. Ltd.

This book contains FSC™ certified paper and other controlled
sources to ensure responsible forest management.

For more information visit: www.harpercollins.co.uk/green

To Rob, Michelle and Sofia,

*A good friend all the way
to the moon and back ...*

CONTENTS

1.   Rover   1

2.   Bunny Hops   8

3.   EARP   15

4.   Oxygen   20

5.   Stranded   27

6.   Photo   32

7.   Tug of War   36

8.   Sea of Luna   42

9.   Lava Tube   48

10. Lander   55

11. Night   61

CHAPTER 1

Rover

"Slow down, Luna!" my father shouts at me as we hit a bump and bounce off the ground. "This Rover *isn't* a race car!"

"Spoilsport!" I reply, and take my foot off the power pedal.

My father gives me a look, but he is grinning as much as I am. "You know I'd be in serious trouble if the Hub commander found out I let you drive. You can easily crash a vehicle on the Moon. There may be very little gravity, but objects still have the same mass, so the Rover will take longer to stop than you think."

"I *did* listen in my Lunar Lessons, Dad," I reply. Even so, I have to brake hard to stop in time for the mine survey spot.

"OK, last rock sample for this trip," says my father, putting on his helmet.

I put mine on too, check my oxygen supply, then open the airlock to the Rover's cabin. Everything goes quiet. In Space, there's no sound. I can only hear the rasp of my breathing inside my helmet – "*Hand me the core sampler, will you?*" – oh, and I can hear my father's rather loud voice over the comms unit too!

I pick up the core sampler. It's a drill with four metal legs that screw into the ground. On Earth I wouldn't be able to lift it. Here, where gravity is six times less, it's as if I've got superpowers! I can easily carry it over to my father.

Dad sets up the core sampler and fixes its feet into the ground. Then he begins to drill

into the Moon rock. I enjoy going on mining
surveys with him. It's fun looking for precious
minerals that we can use for building, turning
into oxygen or making rocket fuel on the Moon.
If we find something, we'll tell the crew at the
Hub that this is a good spot for mining. Best of
all, we get to name the new mine!

It's also good to escape the Hub, where we
live. Yes, the Hub's got air, food, water, TV and

all the other things you need to survive in Space. But it sure is cramped. There are 30 other Moon Miners living there too!

But most of all, the views when you go out on a survey are simply spectacular. It may be the same grey dust and rock everywhere you look. But glance out into Space and you see ...

Earth.

Wow! It's like a big, blue sparkling marble.

There are no stars, of course, because it's daytime right now on the Moon – and about 120 degrees in the sun. That's pretty hot. But don't think I'm taking off my spacesuit any time soon to sunbathe. You have to remember there's little atmosphere on the Moon.

If I took my helmet off, my eyeballs would explode ...

Only joking! They won't explode. And I won't freeze or fry to death, at least not right away. But the oxygen would be sucked from my lungs in just a few seconds. Breathing would be *incredibly* painful. The spit on my tongue would boil away, as well as my blood. (I've been told it's a fizzy feeling like drinking a soda. *Nice, eh?*) But it wouldn't last long. After 15 seconds, I'd pass out and then die from lack of oxygen.

That's why I keep my helmet on.

My visor begins to clatter softly as if it's raining. I frown and look up. There's no rain on the Moon, so what's falling on me?

My comms unit bursts into life. *"Rover 3, return to the Hub right now. Meteorite warning."*

"Let's go!" says my father. "We need to get to cover ASAP!"

We jump into the Rover and my father takes the driving seat. We don't even bother to take off our helmets. He turns the vehicle round and speeds back towards the Hub. We bounce over the lunar surface like some bucking bronco and I have to tighten my seatbelt.

"I thought you said not to drive too fast."

"This must be a big shower for the commander to call us back," Dad says, and grits his teeth. More micro-meteorites batter the windscreen like hail. We crest a small hill and head down slope, picking up speed. In the distance appear a number of large mounds – the Hub.

Then the ground in front of us explodes in a bright flash of dust and rock.

My father swerves to avoid the meteorite strike. But we're going too fast. We hit the impact crater, bounce high and the Rover flips.

CHAPTER 2

Bunny Hops

I open my eyes to see red warning lights flashing across the Rover's dashboard. Through the windscreen the sky appears rock-grey and the Hub is upside down. Then I work out *I'm* the one upside down.

"Are you OK, Luna?" asks my father.

I nod. "Just a little dazed."

"Then let's not hang around."

We unclip our seatbelts and drop to the roof of the cabin, which is now the floor. I land in a slow-motion heap, then crawl outside. The Hub is about 100 metres away. The ground between sends up spurts of dust as it is peppered with micro-meteorites.

My father peers up at the black sky. "That last one was a big 'un. We have to get to shelter before this meteorite shower gets worse."

We run for the Hub. When I say "run", I mean bunny hop at speed. Due to the low gravity, there's a high risk of tripping over a rock or falling flat on your face. The life-support systems on our backs are big and bulky. Also, the lunar dust is very fine and slippery. It's like trying to run on a soft sandy beach in wellies.

Still, with death raining down upon you, it's amazing how fast you *can* move, even on the Moon. As I bound across to the Hub, I must look like Bugs Bunny on a sugar rush! All the way I'm praying we won't get hit by a large, razor-sharp lump of rock that'll rip our

pressure suits. Remember what I told you about my blood boiling? I don't fancy that!

Thankfully, both of us reach the main airlock safely. We dive inside and the door closes behind us. For several seconds it's like we're stood in front of a massive hairdryer as the Moon dust is blown and sucked from our suits.

The "dustbuster", as we call it, hoovers off lunar dirt and stops it entering the Hub. That's important because lunar dirt is rough and sharp like dry coral. The dust clings to everything and can damage equipment. It's also toxic to breathe in. It makes your eyes water and your throat sore, giving you a kind of lunar hay fever. Oh, and in case you want to know, it smells like gunpowder.

The room fills with air and the inner door opens. We're greeted by Rakesh, the Hub's medical officer. "Glad you two made it back. Looked pretty hairy out there."

I take off my helmet. "Nah, it was just a light shower," I reply with a strained smile.

"Well, it's not over just yet," Rakesh says. He turns to my father. "Frank," he says, "Commander Cheng wants to see you."

My father sighs. "Is it about the Rover?"

Rakesh shakes his head. "No, it's more serious than that. She's pretty stressed."

My father stares at Rakesh, then looks at me. "Luna, I'll meet you back at our cabin."

"OK," I reply as my father and Rakesh hurry off towards the central control room.

Why is the commander stressed? She's usually as cool as lunar ice. I don't think the meteorite shower can be the problem. Much of the Hub is under Moon rock and layers of dust to shield it from radiation and micro-meteorites. We should be safe.

I head down the corridor to our cabin, passing fellow Moon Miners along the way. They don't stop to talk, just nod at me and hurry on by. Something's definitely up.

I enter the tiny cabin that my father and I call "home". But the only homey thing in it is a photo of me with my father and mother at our beach house in Cali, Colombia. Our bunkbeds are set into the wall, there's a small table and a wide plastic chair in front of a TV screen, and a tiny shower room with a toilet. That's it.

After all the action, I badly need to go. I hate the nappies we wear under our pressure suits when we're exploring outside. I feel like a little baby and it's *really* gross when the nappy gets wet. That's why I always try to hold it in until I can get back to the Hub.

I dump my helmet on the table, detach my life-support system, peel off my suit and sit down on the toilet. I'm sure you don't want to hear the details. Let's just say, going to the toilet on the Moon is not simple. But it's easier in the Hub than on the space station, which has *zero* gravity. I'll let you work that one out for yourself!

As I sigh with relief, an alarm goes off and flashes red.

Typical! Just as I've started.

CHAPTER 3

EARP

Ever tried putting a pressure suit on in a panic? It's like fighting with a four-legged octopus. I struggle to get my arms and legs into the tight, tough fabric of the suit.

Calm down, Luna! I tell myself.

Eventually I win, connect my life-support system and I'm ready to leave the cabin.

There's no one about, which is a bit weird. I jog along the corridor and poke my head into each room as I pass. Suddenly Science Officer

Brady dashes out of the Hub's lab and almost knocks me over.

"Where's your helmet?" he shouts, and raps his own with his fist.

Idiot, I think. Not Brady, of course. Myself. I forgot my helmet in the cabin.

Training Manual, page 3, paragraph 1. *When the Hub alarm goes, the first action is to put on your pressure suit* – and that *includes* the helmet.

I race back, snatch my helmet off the table and ram it on my head. I lock it into place, then hurry towards the control room – which is our safety zone in an emergency. My feet echo in the empty corridor. *What's happening? Where is everyone?*

I'm starting to feel more than a little alarmed. Then I turn a corner and spot my father sprinting towards me.

"LUNA!" he cries, and waves at me frantically. "We have to evacuate. NOW."

"Where is everyone?" I ask as I rush towards him.

"Already in the EARP."

Now you may be wondering what an EARP is. It's the **EA**rth **R**eturn **P**od. Our emergency escape vehicle. To be used *only* in an emergency. So you'll have worked out – as I'm beginning to – that we're in *serious* danger.

"What's going on, Dad?" I ask, trying not to sound as if I'm panicking (which I am!).

"A stray meteoroid hit one of the Moon's navigation satellites and knocked it out of orbit," my father explains as we run for the control room, which leads to the EARP. "The satellite is on a direct collision course with the Hub. The meteorite shower was just the start. We've less than three minutes before impact—"

A deafening *bang* rocks the Hub, then there's a *roar* of air. I'm yanked off my feet and fly backwards out of the control room. A second later the door to the emergency airlock snaps shut. My father's safe in the control room – and I'm not!

I grab hold of a thick electrical cable running along the wall. As the Hub quickly loses air pressure, I flap around like a kite in a storm. I can see my father's face through the control room window – he's screaming something at me. Then I lose my grip on the cable.

The wind is like a hurricane and pulls me out of the Hub before dumping me on the Moon's rocky ground. I lie there, dazed. A minute later the EARP blasts off from the Hub's launch pad. Its orange-red burners vanish into the black sky like a fading comet.

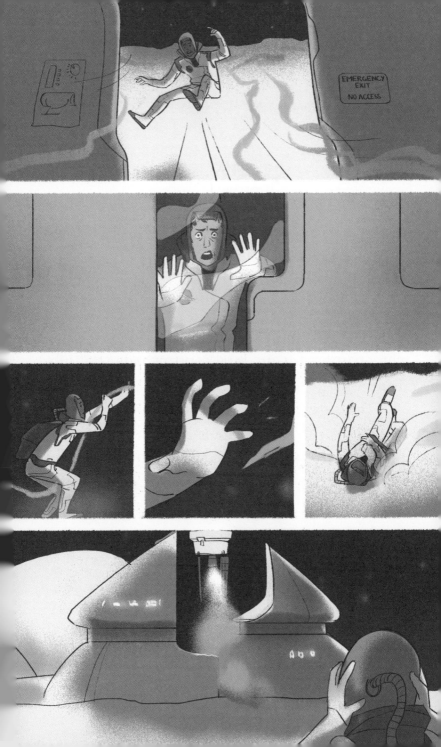

CHAPTER 4

Oxygen

As I watch the EARP leave without me, I see something glinting, hurtling towards the Hub.

The satellite!

Now, if I had a full bladder, my nappy would be getting very, very wet.

I scramble to my feet and bound away. I need to head for cover and there's a small hill not far off. My heart thumps hard in my chest as I dash across the rocky ground.

Halfway to the hill I look back to see the satellite strike the Hub. There's a blinding yet silent flash of an explosion. Rock, dust and debris fly in all directions. I try to duck but I'm hit in the back—

*

I come round to the sound of an alarm beeping.
I'm so cold that I can barely feel my arms or
legs. Still, I wonder why I'm not more dead.
The explosion was huge and the last thing I
remember was being hit by something large
and heavy.

I try to stand – only to find out that I'm
pinned under a door panel from the Hub.
Worse, that beeping alarm is warning me I'm
onto my reserve oxygen tank. The display on
my helmet visor shows that I've less than five
minutes' oxygen supply left. *Great!* Just enough
time to panic, scream for help that won't come,
pity my all-too-short life, then sob loudly before
I take my last breath and die.

But I'm not one to give up so easily.

I push my back hard against the panel. My
arms shake with the effort. At first nothing
happens. But the Moon's lower gravity is on my

side. I perform a press-up worthy of Supergirl and the panel shifts and slides off my back.

I stand up and gaze around. I curse to myself. This long lunar day only gets worse!

The Hub is destroyed. There's a brand-new crater where it used to be. Rubble, rock and sharp splinters of satellite litter the ground. At least the door panel protected me from the worst of the fallout. I guess I should be grateful.

I look up at the empty sky. The EARP is long gone. I just pray my father was on it and is safe. Otherwise—

I gulp back a sob. I can't handle the idea of losing my father so soon after my mother. Then I begin to feel dizzy and I sway on my feet. It's partly from shock but mostly from lack of oxygen. I used up loads of air when I lifted the door panel. My reserve tank is almost empty.

With the Hub gone, I don't have a cosy, oxygen-filled bunker to return to. And the Moon isn't the most welcoming place to survive without air.

Then I spot the crashed Rover. Not keen to die just yet, I stagger over to it. The alarm keeps bleeping loudly in my helmet as I grope for the cabin door and clamber inside. My head pounds and my chest is tight. But I can't take off my helmet yet. I have to wait for the Rover cabin to pressurise.

After a long, painful minute, the light goes green on the Rover's dashboard. I try to unlock my helmet but it's really hard. The lack of oxygen means my fingers won't do what I want them to. I struggle for breath, gasping like a goldfish in a bowl with no water.

Just as I'm about to pass out, I pull my helmet off and gulp in the cabin air at long last. *I'm alive!*

At least for now.

CHAPTER 5

Stranded

The problem is ... no one knows I'm still alive.

My father and the rest of the Moon Miners will think I was killed in the explosion. The satellite was travelling at well over 15,000 kilometres per hour and hit the ground like a bomb. Just look for yourself ... it punched a crater 20 metres wide!

Even I can't believe I wasn't crushed into lunar dust.

But somehow I survived. *Woo hoo!* Shame I can't tell anyone the happy news.

The Hub's satellite dish is destroyed. The Rover's comms unit is dead too. I've tested it – the antenna is crushed and broken under the Rover.

I sit cross-legged on the roof of the cabin that is now my floor and think about the mess I'm in.

I'm stranded on the Moon. With nowhere to live, nothing to eat or drink and no means of communication. Even if I could contact someone, any hope of rescue is at least three days and 400,000 kilometres away!

All of a sudden it hits me that I'm the *only* living person on this lump of grey rock. I've always been a bit of a loner – especially after my mum died – but this is going a little too far.

And soon I'll be the only *dead* person on this lump of grey rock.

You'll be happy to know though that I wasn't sent to the Moon totally unprepared. Every Moon Miner – kids too – has to do six months of intensive training. I learned useful things like the effects of lower gravity, how to use a core sampler and what to do in an emergency.

The first and best option is to escape back to Earth on the EARP.

If that doesn't happen (*ha!*), we were told the five key elements for survival on the Moon are oxygen, water, food, power and pressurised shelter.

The last one is the easiest to solve right now. Along with my pressure suit, I have the Rover. It's pretty much a campervan for the Moon and the cabin is fully pressurised. The seats lie flat to make beds and there's a store of essential supplies. The Rover allows a Moon Miner to explore for up to four Earth days away from the Hub.

I do a quick stock check. This solves three more survival elements. At least for the time being.

I have enough water and food packs for about two Earth days. The Rover would normally have more but my father and I had already been out on the survey trip.

There's also oxygen (*yay!*) but not much of it (*boo!*). The Rover itself has two large tanks. They were half used up by the time we got back to the Hub and one has been damaged in the crash. I reckon I've two, maybe three Earth days' supply at most.

Good news is that I've found three spare oxygen tanks for my life-support system. That should give me another day – if I don't breathe too much (*ha!*).

The main problem is power. Both the Hub and the Rover use solar panels to charge their batteries. The Hub's panels have been buried by the fallout from the satellite strike. And the ones on the roof of the Rover now face the ground, not the sun.

I look off to the horizon. Night is drawing in.

But not just yet. I've got at least another 48 hours, that is two more Earth days, before the sun sets. You see, a lunar day lasts about one Earth month or 700 hours. In other words, two weeks of sun, followed by two weeks of darkness. As I no longer have the Hub's back-up batteries, that means no power in sub-zero temperatures of minus 230 degrees.

That is not a happy thought.

CHAPTER 6

Photo

I guess this must be how the crew of the Apollo 13 mission felt after the oxygen tank on their spacecraft exploded halfway to the Moon. Desperate ... but determined not to give up.

Well, if three middle-aged men can overcome impossible odds to survive in Space and return safely to Earth, I can too.

I just need a few more supplies, a little inventiveness and a load of luck.

I clip a new oxygen tank on my life-support system, exit the cabin and take a look at the

Rover. Apart from being upside down, it's intact and appears drivable. I try to roll it back over onto its wheels. But it's no good. Even on the Moon, with almost no gravity, there's no way I can turn the Rover the right way up again.

So I leave that little problem for later and explore what's left of the Hub. It's not a pretty sight. The control room, lab and EARP launch pad have been smashed into a rocky crater. The greenhouse has been flattened – all the plants dead. Most depressing of all, the oxygen generator and power station are both destroyed and beyond repair.

That's the bad news.

The good news is that some parts of the Hub survived. In the half-buried storeroom, there's a box of Hub food, two full bags of water and, joy of joys, a pack of premium astronaut nappies! So I can now eat, drink *and* wee for a few extra days – that could be the difference between life and death.

I don't mean going to the toilet; I mean surviving long enough to be rescued!

In the wreck of the Hub's workshop, I find two sets of solar panels. I also dig up one of those core sampler drills that we use on mining surveys, and a reel of titanium cable. I click my fingers – or at least I try to (it isn't easy with a spacesuit on) – I have a plan!

As I sift through the rest of the wreckage for anything else that might be useful, I spot a bright burst of colour against the grey dust of the Moon. I stop dead. It's the photo of me and my parents at our beach house. I can't believe it survived the impact.

I smile sadly. The photo is my last happy memory of all three of us together. My father and I applied for the Moon-mining mission after my mum died. The space agency wanted to test the effects of lunar living on children. They were looking for families who would be happy to spend time on the Moon. We knew the risks.

But you have to understand, life on Earth wasn't fun for us any more and the Moon felt like a good place to escape to.

That was then.

Now I'm on a mission to *escape* the Moon.

I make a silent vow to my dead mother and the father I hope is still alive that I *will* get back home. I bend down to pick up the photo. It crumbles between my fingers like ash.

Not a good omen.

CHAPTER 7

Tug of War

Have you heard of Sir Isaac Newton? He was the seventeenth-century English scientist who came up with the theory of gravity after an apple was said to have fallen on his head. He also developed the Three Laws of Motion. I learned about these in my lunar lessons. They're important for understanding and predicting how things move in space.

The first law says that an object at rest will stay at rest, and an object that is moving will keep moving, **unless** an external force acts on it, such as a push or a pull.

Let's put that law to the test. The Rover is currently not moving – it's stuck on its roof and will stay that way unless *I* do something about it. So I take the core sampler I found in the Hub workshop and set it up five metres away from the Rover. I screw its legs into the ground, then tie one end of the titanium cable to the sampler's drill bit and the other to the Rover's wheelbase.

This is where I test out Newton's First Law and try to get the still object to move.

I switch on the core sampler. The drill bit turns and slowly coils the cable around it. As the slack is taken up, a tug of war begins between the sampler and the Rover. I only hope the cable's strong enough. But I really needn't worry. After all, it's made of titanium. I should be more worried about the sampler. As the Rover is pulled up onto its side, I notice the sampler's legs are working loose from the ground.

I forgot Newton's Third Law of Motion. For every action, there is an equal and opposite reaction. In other words, as the core sampler pulls the Rover one way, the Rover is pulling the sampler the other way. And because the Rover has greater mass than the drill, it should win the tug of war.

Without thinking what I am doing, I jump onto the sampler, grab hold of its legs and stand on top of its metal feet. This is very risky. If the Rover wins, I'll be flung into Space. But my added weight is just enough for the core sampler to win the tug of war. At the last second, the Rover rolls over in a slow-motion bellyflop and lands on its wheels.

I leap off the sampler in a bunny hop of delight. One problem solved!

Now I have food, water, shelter *and* transport. Next I have to sort out some means of communication.

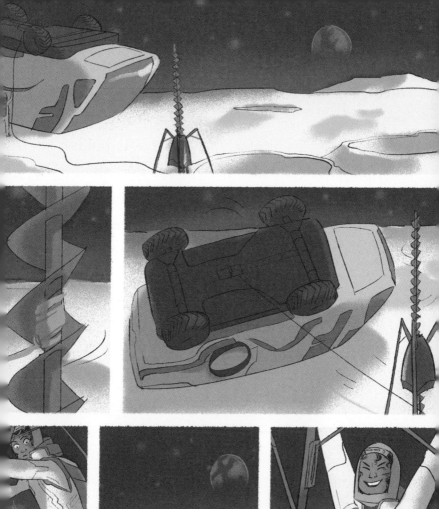

I guess I could write HELP in gigantic letters in the dust and hope a passing astronaut spots it!

I laugh to myself. Then stop. Maybe that's not a bad idea after all. I mean, the space agency will send an observation module or at least turn a telescope to survey the damaged Hub. The key question is when? And will they do it before the lunar night falls and everything is hidden by the dark?

I can't rely on that happening in time. My best bet is to get the Rover's comms unit working. I clamber aboard and do a systems check. The Rover's batteries are half full. But that's no longer a problem as I now have the two sets of solar panels to recharge them. The electrical system shows no faults. And the comms unit seems to be working fine. There's just no signal.

I need a new antenna. But where will I get one of those on the Moon? I can't simply go out and buy one. And I didn't come across a spare in the wrecked workshop. Nor do I have the skill to make or repair one.

I slump in my seat and stare at the digital map of the lunar landscape on the Rover's console. It's pretty bleak out there. Just like my options.

Right at the top of the map there's an icon of a small footprint marking the Armstrong Memorial in the Sea of Tranquillity. Maybe one day there'll be a memorial to me. Instead of "First Man to Land on the Moon", it will say "First Girl to Be Stranded on the Moon".

That's when I spot another tiny image next to it that looks like a small insect. The icon for a Moon-lander.

"For Lunar sake!" I cry. I sit up fast as an idea flashes across my mind like a shooting star.

CHAPTER 8

Sea of Luna

Over the years of lunar exploration, there have been more than twenty landers sent from Earth to the surface of the Moon. Most of them were unmanned. But each one has an antenna to communicate with Earth. Many, like Armstrong's lander, touched down near the equator of the Moon. That's too far away to be any help to me. It would take weeks to reach them.

But one – Surveyor 7 – landed just north of Tycho crater.

Having plotted a course, the Rover calculates it will take me a little less than two Earth days to get to Surveyor 7. I'll need to stop at least once to sleep and to allow the Rover batteries to recharge. With the lunar night closing in, that'll be cutting it fine. But this may be my best shot.

I know that survival experts tell you to stay near any accident site, since there's a bigger chance of you being found if you do. But I don't have the time to wait and be found.

I hook up the solar panels and leave the Rover to charge. Then I load the supplies I collected into the back of the Rover. After that, I lay out rocks and any wreckage I can lift to spell out HELP on the ground.

I stand back to admire my work. The word is clear but will it be big enough? All I can say is that the space agency will need a darn good telescope to read it!

My last job is to write a note on the panel door that saved me after the satellite crash, just in case rescue arrives while I'm away. I give the coordinates of Surveyor 7, my planned route, the time of my departure and my estimated arrival. As I sign off my name with a jokey "*Race you there!*", it hits me how risky my plan actually is. This is a one-way trip. I won't be coming back.

With a last nervous look at the ruins of the Hub, I board the Rover.

I've got a long drive ahead.

*

After eight hours, I come to a stop. The Rover's batteries are almost drained. Mine are too. I can't keep my eyes open. Also, between you and me, I *really* need a change of nappy.

Once that's been dealt with, I exit the cabin and lay out the solar panels. The sun's strong rays should charge up the Rover in just a few hours.

I peer off towards the rim of Tycho crater in the distance. So far I've made good progress. And if I'm honest with you, I'm quite enjoying the drive. Yes, the terrain is rough and my life is at risk. But it's exciting to think that I'm the first girl – in fact, first human – to have ever made such a long, solo journey on the Moon.

Having driven across part of the southern highlands, I've reached the edge of a sea. It isn't a sea, by the way. There's almost no water on the Moon. Only buried ice at the north and south poles. The seas are actually ancient lava fields covered in Moon dust. The one I'm looking at now is pretty small and isn't named on the map.

So I'm going to call it the *Sea Of Luna*.

To mark it as my own, I step out onto its untouched surface and plant my boot in the soft dust. I grin as I leave a perfect footprint.

"Beat that, Armstrong!" I whisper.

Then I return to the Rover and lay the driver's seat flat. The makeshift bed isn't very comfy, but I'm so tired I could sleep on Moon rock. As I drift off, I gaze at the Earth hanging like a blue jewel in the sky. I wonder if the EARP has docked with the Gateway space station yet ... *Is my father there? Is he safe?*

*

A loud bleep wakes me. The Rover's batteries are fully charged. Yawning, I put on my helmet, go outside and collect in the solar panels. Then I climb back into the driver's seat.

Ahead of me lies my *Sea of Luna*. Once across, I'll be at the base of Tycho crater and near the lander at last. Keen to get going, I press the power pedal to the floor and the Rover lurches forward.

The going is faster and smoother on the sea. I drive another eight hours solid, stop to recharge and sleep, and then set off again. I'm making good time when an unexpected sight brings me to a standstill.

On the far side of the sea, a steep cliff blocks my way.

CHAPTER 9

Lava Tube

On the map, the cliff is only a thin line, a low ridge running from the rim of Tycho crater. But in reality it is a long, high wall of rock. There's no way on earth – or should I say the Moon – the Rover can climb that.

I instruct the Rover to plot another route. No good. I would have to drive all the way around the cliff and circle the crater to reach the lander. Direct, the lander is less than an hour's drive away. But this new route would take another full Earth day. And I only have six hours of sunlight left.

I gaze at the cliff and the rim of Tycho crater beyond. *So close yet so far!* I thump the dashboard with my fist. I'm never going to get to the lander. Might as well give up now ...

Then, as I look along the cliff's vast length, I spot a large, dark hole at its base. *A lava tube!*

My father told me about these tunnels. They were formed during eruptions millions of years ago. These tubes can be up to 300 metres wide. The space agency are interested in them because the tunnels could be used for Moon bases ... or mining sites ... or even underground roads.

And an underground road is exactly what I need. This lava tube could lead through the cliff to the lander!

Then again, it could be a dead end.

But I have to take that chance. If I try the other route, I end up dead anyway.

I turn on the headlights and drive into the lava tube. The Rover is swallowed up by the huge hole. The tunnel is about 20 metres wide, pitch-black and terrifying. Razor-sharp spikes of cooled lava hang down from the ceiling and the floor is all rippled and ropy. It's like entering the belly of an alien monster.

The tunnel goes on and on, sloping upwards. Sometimes it curves left, then right, but mostly straight. After an hour of slow, careful

driving, I reckon I must be near to the lander site, but I'm still underground. *When will this tunnel end?*

The Rover bleeps a warning. Its batteries are running low. I should have recharged before I entered the lava tube. That was stupid! I now have a difficult choice: press on or turn back.

My headlights pick out nothing ahead. Just tunnel and more tunnel.

The thought of dying in the lava tube, in the pitch-dark, where no one will ever find me, is awful. I decide to turn around.

But the Rover's engine cuts out and I lose all power.

Oh, come on! Don't fail me now.

I try to restart the engine. Nothing happens.

As I sit in the darkness, scared and alone, I begin to notice a faint glow reflecting off the tunnel's walls. *Sunlight?*

Could we be near the end of the tunnel? The thought gives me hope. I turn off the cabin's heater and all non-vital systems, and re-route any power that's left direct to the engine. The Rover blinks back to life.

I drive slowly forward. As I turn the corner, I am greeted by a large bright circle of light. The end of the lava tube!

I come out onto the flat plain near the rim of Tycho crater. Less than 200 metres away sits a Moon-lander.

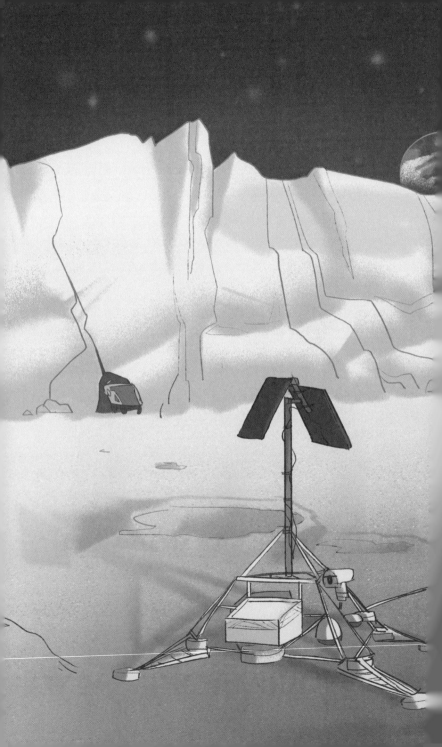

CHAPTER 10

Lander

The lander is an antique. And that's being kind to it. Surveyor 7 is ready for the scrap heap.

It's coated in years of lunar dust, its skeletal frame looks frail and weak. The tech is so old and basic I worry nothing will work. In fact, I fear that Surveyor 7 will fall apart if I even touch it.

I find the main control unit and carefully take off the panel with an electric screwdriver. I'm not a technical wiz but I do understand the basics of a circuit board. I look for where the wires to the antenna and battery are attached,

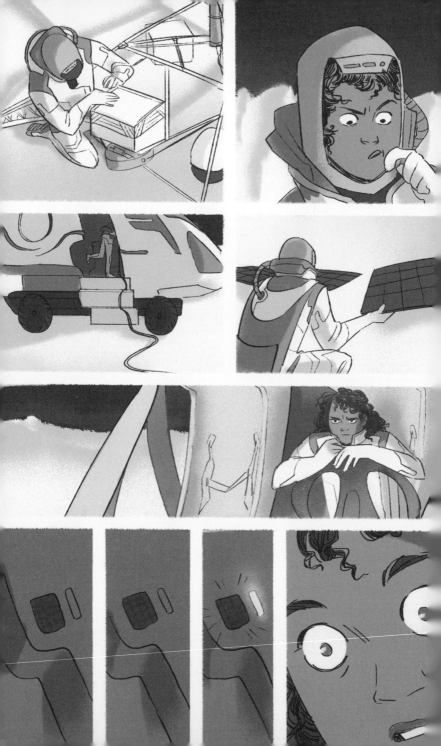

then I link these to the Rover's computer system.

I need to both power and control the lander. So my first task is to lay out the Rover's solar panels for a final charge before night falls in less than five hours. Next, I'm counting on the Rover's AI program to figure out how to talk to the lander.

With the Rover and lander linked, I clamber back into the cabin and switch on the power. The lander just sits there like a massive dead stick insect.

I chew my lip as the minutes pass. Come on, work! Then a small LED light blinks on like an eye. *Surveyor 7 is alive!*

I turn on the comms unit. All I can get is a harsh crackle of static. Then I spot the problem – the antenna is out of position. I instruct the Rover to line it up with Earth.

At first nothing happens. The two systems must be speaking in different computer codes. But the Rover is quick to adapt. All of a sudden the lander jerks into life, the antenna shifts to the left and a beep sounds from the comms unit.

My voice is trembling as I speak into the microphone. "Luna to Mission Control, are you reading me?"

Silence.

"Luna to Mission Control, *anyone* there?"

More silence.

I guess the answer is no. It seems my gamble didn't pay off. I blink back tears and try not to collapse into a sobbing heap. *Sorry, Mum and Dad, I did my best to get home alive.*

Oh well, it was a nice road trip while it lasted. And I must now have the record for the longest solo journey on the Moon. Maybe my name will go down in the history books, who knows—

A burst of static cuts in on my morbid thoughts. I hear a woman's voice on the comms unit. "Reading you ... Luna ... This is Gateway ... Where are you?"

I jump to my feet, hitting my head on the ceiling. "Tycho crater!" I cry.

"How did you ever get *there?*" The woman on Earth's Gateway space station sounds shocked.

"I drove," I reply, and quickly detail my journey. Several rapid questions follow. After I've given the Earth Gateway space station my exact location, oxygen levels, battery status and supply situation, someone I know takes over the comms – my father.

"Luna, you're alive!"

"Surprise!" I reply, and at last I can let myself truly smile. He's alive too!

"We're coming to rescue you, Luna," he says. "Stay right where you are."

I can't help but laugh. "Where else am I going to go, Dad?"

CHAPTER 11

Night

Night falls. Fast and hard. One moment there is sun. The next, darkness.

But I don't panic. Rescue is coming.

I have supplies to last me two more days, and if I'm careful with the Rover's batteries, I should be able to heat the cabin so that I don't freeze to death.

Out of the sunlight, the Moon's surface will soon drop to a chilly minus 230 degrees. But on the plus side, I can now see the stars. Billions of them.

The sky looks like a blanket of glistening diamonds. Every one a sun in its own right.

I told you the view on the Moon is spectacular :-)

This is Luna ... signing off for the night ...

Our books are tested
for children and young people by
children and young people.

Thanks to everyone who consulted on
a manuscript for their time and effort in
helping us to make our books better
for our readers.